I0788384

Written and Illustrated
by
Takeya Trayer
the night before
XMAS

Takeya Trayer

BROTHERLY LOVE IS
LOVE BETWEEN
EQUALS: BUT INDEED,
EVEN AS EQUALS WE
ARE NOT ALWAYS
"EQUAL"; INASMUCH
AS WE ARE HUMAN, WE
ARE ALL IN NEED OF
HELP. TODAY I.
TOMORROW YOU.
-ERICH FROMM

To my kings Aziz and Kyerim,
from a very proud parent. We
grow, we learn, we love and
laugh.

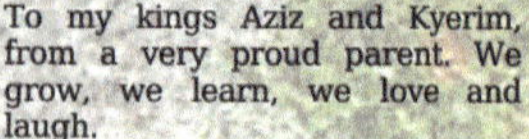

Published

by TakeYaArt LLC

First Edition PRINT
August 2025
ISBN978-1-7372850-4-5

PRESIDENT TAKEYA TRAYER
EDITOR KYERIM TRAYER
ASSISTANT EDITOR AZIZ TRAYER
DESIGNER TAKEYA TRAYER
DESIGN EDITOR KYERIM AND AZIZ TRAYER
DIGITAL EDITOR TAKEYA TRAYER

ILLUSTRATIONS TAKEYA TRAYER
INTERIOR AND COVER DESIGNER
TAKEYA TRAYER

DESCRIPTION: famille familia famiglia,
biodiversity
IDENTIFIERS:
ISBN978-1-7372850-4-5 (Hardback)

MORE INFORMATION AT WWW.TAKEYAART.COM

ABOUT THE AUTHOR

My first self-published book, My Mommy Is My Daddy, came from that period. I illustrated it with my non-dominant hand, mimicking the innocent style I saw in my children's drawings. Later, with a grant from Creative Pinellas in Florida, I re-released the book in color with cut paper collage illustrations. Collage, to me, speaks to life's layers—raw, textured, imperfect, and real.

My work spans mediums and geographies: painting exhibitions and spoken word in Pennsylvania, fashion and fine art in California, collage, puppetry, and stop motion animation in Florida. In 2024, I was awarded a residency with Greenbook and exhibited in St. Pete's WADA district. I also joined the Arts Annual at Creative Pinellas and connected with WeArt for mentorship.

Currently my creativity is thriving and I am attempting to reimagine my unfinished work. I'm inspired by traditional and futuristic ways of making, sharing, and interacting with art—seeking not just to express, but to connect and engage on a deeper level.

Born in Pennsylvania to interracial parents, a DNA test later revealed my roots to be even more global than I imagined. I've always felt like a child of the world. Before becoming a parent, my art was bold, dramatic, and provocative—but in hindsight, it lacked the depth that helps art to be engaging and resonant over time. Being a parent has led me to noticing more subtleties in myself, others and the natural world around me. That realization of imperfections is also a realization of diversity that is intricately woven. The metaphors hold truths creatively.

In 2010, after the birth of my first child, I received the Art and Change Award from the Leeway Foundation in Philadelphia. That support allowed me to write books and scripts, and mount a solo show—all while raising my children at home. It was a time of joy and relentless creativity, despite limited resources.

Takeya Trayer

FOREWORD

The Night Before Xmas is a modern day tribute to a one hundred year old poem "The Night Before Christmas," by Clement Clarke Moore. That poem has popularized the many aspects that we celebrate during the Christmas Holiday. As our present day Christmas realizes into something vastly different than what it originated as we should reimagine those changes in our stories. The images and interpretations of Santa (Klaus) in the book represent the growing variations of an interpopulated multicultural society. Trayer's version The Night Before Xmas is consciously designed to be as inclusive as it is satirical. It paradoxically is anti discriminatory showing that online shopping doesn't care what ethnicity, culture, religion you're from, it's open for you. While also sharing a message of being open and accepting of others. The eclectic cut out style illustrations used are magazine, newsprint and museum inspired. The idyllic illustrations are created from digitally edited hand drawn images, AI enhanced backgrounds and paper collage. The combination of traditional art methods and futuristic help imply what the current human population is devoted to. The poem is original, written and adapted by Takeya Trayer, not AI generated.

MORE INFORMATION AT WWW.TAKEYAART.COM
@T@KEY@@RT
@TAKEYAART

Twas the night before xmas
when all through the loft,
not a sound could be heard
not even a cough.
The stockings were hung on
the mantle with care
in hopes that in the morning
they still would be there.

WHAT KIND OF
DECORATIONS DO
YOU USE DURING
YOUR HOLIDAY?

CAN ANIMALS HAVE CELEBRATIONS?

DO YOU REMEMBER YOUR DREAMS?

The children were nestled all snug in their beds,
While visions of devices played in their heads.
Mamma in her nighty and I in my flannel,
had just rock paper scissored to decide on a channel.

SHINE BRIGHT
LIKE A DIAMOND

HAVE YOU EVER
MADE A GIVING
ROCK?

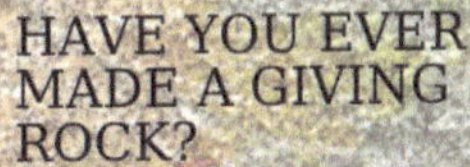

When out in the yard arouse such a fuss.
I sprang into action to tell them to hush.
Away to the window I flew in a flutter,
threw open the curtains and raised up
the shutter.

IF YOUR GLASSES
HAD SPECIAL
POWERS WHAT
WOULD THEY BE?

The moonlight poured like rain
from the sky
and made it seem like I was the
only thing dry.
When what to my digital specs did
appear,
a delivery gem surrounded by deer.

WHAT DOES YOUR
NAME MEAN TO
YOU?

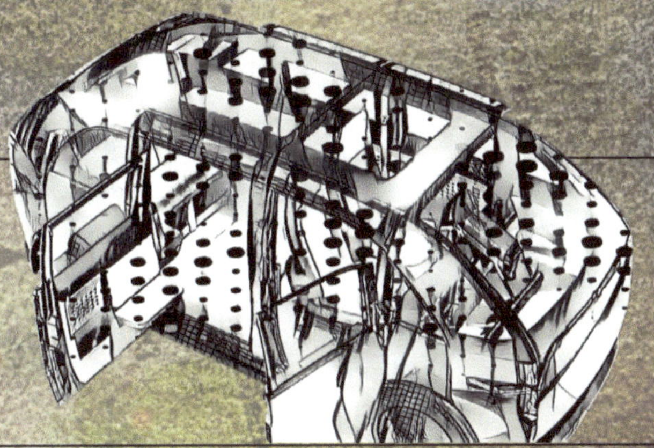

With a hesitant look
so bashful yet proud
they carried some
packages stealth
through the crowd.
I zoomed in to read
Nix on their tag
as they made their
way to my door with
a zig and a zag.

PARKOUR MEANS

THE ACTIVITY OR SPORT OF MOVING RAPIDLY THROUGH AN AREA, TYPICALLY IN AN URBAN ENVIRONMENT.
-OXFORD -

Nix lowered their bundle,
the deer raised their brow.
They pointed their finger upward
and gave them a bow.
Dasher, Dancer, Prancer and Vixen
And Comet and Cupid and Donner and Blitzen
had trained many years
in the art of Parkour.
Because there is nothing more boring
than using the door.

NAMASTE MEANS   A SANSKRIT WORD MEANING "I BOW TO YOU" AND USED AS A GREETING.

Without blinking an eye I felt so aloof.
In seconds I heard the hoofs on the roof.
I drew my head in and was turning around when
I was startled by the incredible sound.
Of the tumbling chimney and shaking mantle,
I rushed down the stairs as I blew out the candle.

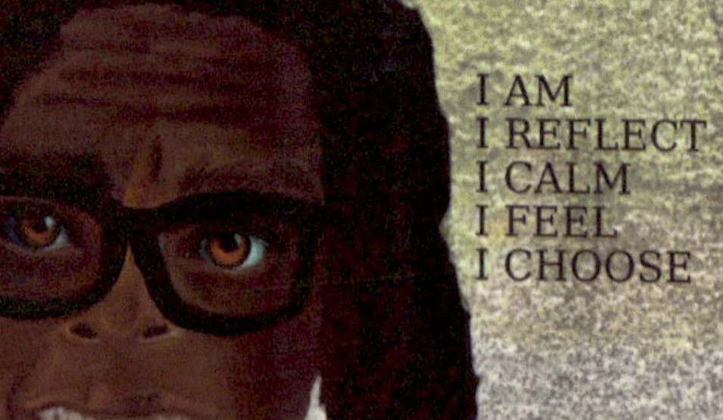

**And there stood Nix
grinning and cheesing
and shining and glowing
for no kind of reason.
Teeming with life
from their head to their
feet,
their clothes were a bit
dusty with soot, ash and
sleet.**

I AM
I REFLECT
I CALM
I FEEL
I CHOOSE

DUST YOUR
SHOULDERS
OFF AND …

A bundle of packages
slung on their back,
they gobbled a cookie and
began to unpack.
This gem how expressive,
their face did perspire.
Their plush eyebrows
united, their eyes did not
tire.

C IS FOR COOKIE

Their cheeks were all flushed, their
nose Egyptian and strong.
Their mouth exercised as their lips
whistled along.
Nix was clean cut and shaven but their
hair was a mess.
It was obvious that Nix
did not like to rest.

I NOTICED YOUR BODY MOVING ALL AROUND SO I THINK YOU WILL REALLY LIKE THIS SONG. (MAKE UP A SONG TOGETHER)

both male and female
reindeer or caribou
(Rangifer tarandus)
grow antlers

Their soul was so youthful and spirit so bright.
Frozen, I could do nothing but stare in delight.
With a wink of their eye and a nod of their head,
gave me relief to know that I had nothing to dread.

HOW CAN YOU COMMUNICATE WITHOUT TALKING?

What is your favorite thing to learn with your family?

They filled all the stockings
and the pups did not stir.
They left each doggie a treat
and patted their fur.
Emptied the bundle right and
left of the mantle
and on the Menorah, Nix lit the
first candle.

What kind of
treats are for
doggies?

Light luz lumen
is a common
theme in
celebrations,
representing
joy growth
warmth
pureness.

WHY MUST WE
TAKE OUR
TIME?

I must have had great
questioning eyes,
because they turned
directly to
acknowledge surprise.
Their gaze telepathic,
the communication,
so slight.
I celebrate everything,
I celebrate life.

"MAY YOU ALWAYS FIND WATER AND SHADE,
AND MAY THE WHEEL OF TIME NEVER CEASE
TO TURN" -ROBERT JORDAN

How do you fill a heart with love?

DO YOU HAVE A FAVORITE PAIR OF SHOES?
DRAW THOSE SHOES DANCING WALKING PARKOUR

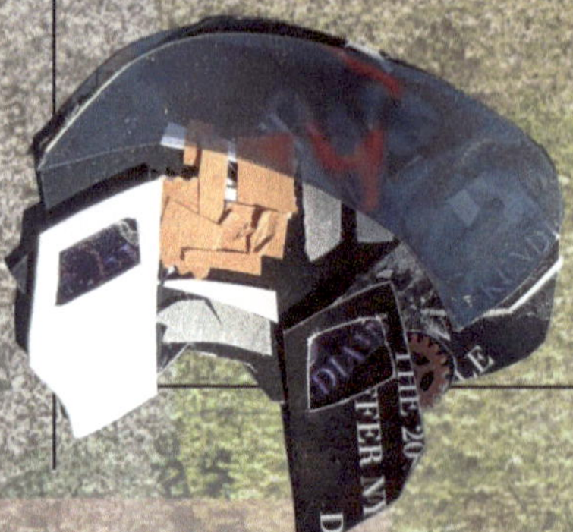

Up the chimney they rose
without scaling the bricks.
They sprang to the truck
sporting the latest new kicks.
I ran through the loft my
heart filled with love,
to watch Nix depart from
the window above.

Coordinates entered for the next destination, the team close behind awaiting location.

COORDINATION
COOPERATION
COMMUNICATION

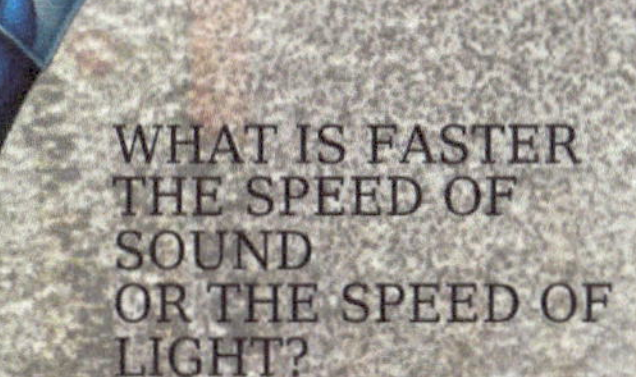

WHAT IS FASTER
THE SPEED OF
SOUND
OR THE SPEED OF
LIGHT?

**The engine fired up with that clean energy sound.
It evenly lifted in place and hovered the ground.
It looked like a truck but flew like a drone.
Nix connected to bluetooth at the sound of the tone.**

WHAT IS A
HOVERCRAFT?

Do you need a
license to fly a
drone? Draw a drone
license for Santa and
include their portrait.

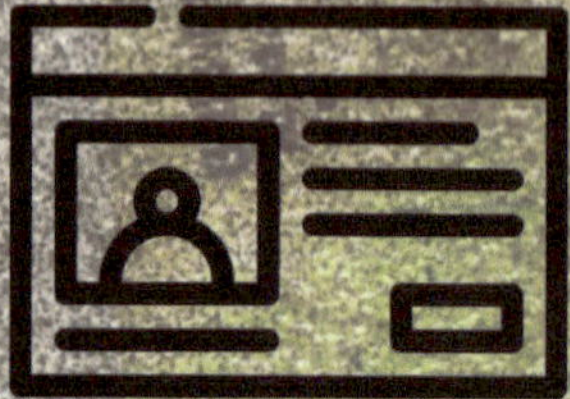

GIVE THESE DEER
NEW NAMES.

I heard Nix exclaim as they vanished from sight,
I'm in the business of gifts for more than one night!

WHAT KIND OF GIFTS DO YOU ENJOY RECEIVING?

What kind of gifts do you enjoy giving?

The End.

What did I miss?

Whatever you believe
in, whatever you
celebrate may you
operate with
care, responsibility
respect and knowledge